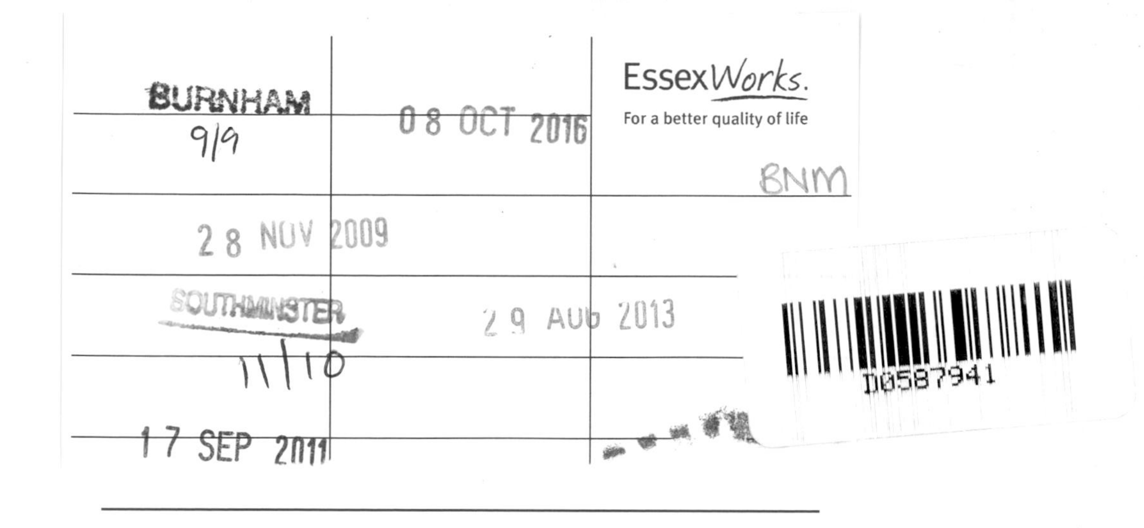
EssexWorks.
For a better quality of life
BNM
BURNHAM
9/9
08 OCT 2016
28 NOV 2009
SOUTHMINSTER
29 AUG 2013
11/10
17 SEP 2011
D0587941

30130 163470585

For Conrad

E. D.

First published in Great Britain in 2008 by Gullane Children's Books.
This paperback edition published in 2009 by

Gullane Children's Books
185 Fleet Street, London, EC4A 2HS
www.gullanebooks.com

1 3 5 7 9 10 8 6 4 2

Text and Illustrations © Emma Dodd 2008

The right of Emma Dodd to be identified as the author and illustrator of this work has been asserted by her in accordance with the Copyright, Designs and Patents Act, 1988.
A CIP record for this title is available from the British Library.

ISBN: 978-1-86233-753-4

All rights reserved. No part of this publication may be reproduced, stored in a retrieval system, or transmitted in any form or by any means electronic, mechanical, photocopying, recording or otherwise, without prior permission.

Printed and bound in Indonesia

Best Bear

Emma Dodd

Day's end,
time for bed.
Cuddle up
best Ted.

Worn fur,
kissed away.
Was white
now grey.

Button eye,
patchwork nose,
places where
stuffing shows.

Old bear,
many mends.
We are
best friends.

Toys, toys
everywhere.
Only one
special bear!

All alone, dark night.
Snuggle down, squeeze tight.

What's that
by the door?
Shapes loom.
Hold your paw.

Any monsters
don’t dare,
come near
MY bear.

You're brave,
me too.
Scared of the dark?
Not with you!

Safe, sound, warm, cosy.
Start to feel a little dozy.

Wonder what tomorrow brings?
Lots and lots of lovely things.

Night's here,
sleep time.
I'm yours
you're mine!

Other Gullane Children's Books for you to enjoy . .

This is the Way
Charles Fuge

Penguins
Liz Pichon

I Love You Always and Forever
Jonathan Emmet
illustrated by Daniel Howarth

What Can a Baby Do?
Sarah Churchill
illustrated by Charles Fuge